MW00748224

ST A... ...IS C...
01...

A Winter for Leo

A Winter for Leo

by Nicole Leroux

translated by Sheila Fischman

illustrated by Sophie Lewandowski

Harper*Trophy*Canada™
An imprint of HarperCollins*PublishersLtd*

A Winter for Leo

Copyright © Éditions du Boréal, Montréal, 2003
English translation © 2006 by Sheila Fischman.
All rights reserved.

Published by Harper*Trophy*Canada™, an imprint of HarperCollins Publishers Ltd

No part of this book may be used or reproduced in any manner whatsoever without the prior written permission of the publisher, except in the case of brief quotations embodied in reviews.

Harper*Trophy*Canada™ is a trademark of HarperCollins Publishers.

First English-language edition. Originally published in French by Éditions du Boréal under the title *L'Hiver de Léo Polatouche*.

HarperCollins books may be purchased for educational, business, or sales promotional use through our Special Markets Department.

HarperCollins Publishers Ltd
2 Bloor Street East, 20th Floor
Toronto, Ontario, Canada
M4W 1A8

www.harpercollins.ca

Library and Archives Canada Cataloguing in Publication
Leroux, Nicole
[Hiver de Léo Polatouche. English]
A winter for Leo / Nicole Leroux ; translated by Sheila Fischman.

Translation of L'hiver de Léo Polatouche.
ISBN-13: 978-0-00-639582-9
ISBN-10: 0-00-639582-1

I. Fischman, Sheila II. Title.

PS8573.E672H5813 2006   JC843'.6   C2006-902426-X

Illustrations: Sophie Lewandowski, colagene.com

HC 9 8 7 6 5 4 3 2

Printed and bound in the United States

Contents

CHAPTER 1   The Runaway

CHAPTER 2   Waiting

CHAPTER 3   A Place to Stay

CHAPTER 4   Disaster

CHAPTER 5   The New House

CHAPTER 6   What a Strange Way to Live!

CHAPTER 7   Outside at Last

CHAPTER 8   Leo's Talents

CHAPTER 9   Doctor Ermine Comes Back

CHAPTER 10   A Weight on the Heart

CHAPTER 11   Big News!

CHAPTER I

The Runaway

His father's anger was still growling in his ears.

"A fiasco, that's what it is, a real fiasco!"

Those were the harsh words he'd spat out as the troupe gathered up the dangling wires. His father had pointed at him. And his mother . . . Leo could see the disappointment in her eyes. A good-for-nothing. That's what they thought about him, about Leo Polatouche the Acrobat.

His mind was made up. He wasn't going

to spend one more minute on this house-boat. He was going away forever, and his parents and his brothers and his sisters would be sorry that they'd made fun of him and been mean to him.

After the show, Leo took his bag out from under his bed, hoisted it over his shoulder — though he didn't know what to put in it — and sneaked off the houseboat. On the shore, under the tall trees where they had put on the show, he paced furi-ously back and forth for a long time. Every-thing was all mixed up. He was as agitated as their floating house when it bobbed up and down on stormy days when the wind was strong.

He looked back at what was their home. It was secure and solid and the family of fly-ing squirrels was snug. Leo felt very alone. Right now all the lamps were lit. He rec-ognized every one of the shadows moving around behind the thin curtains at the portholes. How sad! No one had even noticed his absence. Probably they'd all be glad that he had disappeared. Good riddance.

He headed toward the big oak tree and sat beneath it. Picking up a small branch, he started to scrape the ground. He drew his own likeness in the soft soil. Anyway, he, Leo, would never set foot on that houseboat again. Never!

"They can all go to the devil!"

Inside his head he started shrieking words full of anger. He would be happy if he never saw them again.

Still, there was Grandpa, who didn't make fun of him, who loved him. From where Leo was sitting he could see the big poster on the wall of the kitchen in the cabin: THE FAMILY POLATOUCHE — HIGH WIRE ARTISTS.

The rest of them could walk on the high wire and turn somersaults on the flying trapeze — without a net. But it was hopeless. He, Leo, simply could not do it. Even though he trained day in and day out and worked so hard. The problem was that paw of his! The bad paw, the wretched thing that hadn't grown normally. It was why he couldn't balance himself on the high wire.

And his mother was always telling him: "Eat, eat!"

Food had nothing to do with it though. The problem was his paw and his size. Even though he ate as much as the others, he could see that he would always be smaller than his sister, who'd been born long after him. He was different.

It had been the last show before winter and nothing could change what had happened. There had been so many snags: "a fiasco, a real fiasco." Leo felt ashamed, humiliated. The forest streams would soon be frozen. His parents would take the houseboat to a little corner safe from the wind. With their home solidly moored and covered with branches and leaves, they would be cozy and warm all winter. The houseboat would serve as a big nest. Leo wouldn't live that life anymore. They'd have to do their somersaults without him.

Leo wrapped himself in his woollen cape and covered his head with the hood. It was going to be a cold night. The sun had set a while ago. Inside the house, with the lanterns lit behind the curtains, it looked like their wintertime shadow theatre when Leo's family made up stories.

Leo had grown up on that houseboat. When the weather was fine, the family travelled along the waterways. Place after place, his father dropped anchor and made fast the houseboat. They settled near clearings that were easily approachable. Once the boat was moored, the biggest children would scout around for a suitable place to put up the trapezes and the high wires. His father or his grandfather would ask the section head's permission to set up there. Usually, by the next evening before dusk, the family would give a performance — sometimes two — in exchange for a few coins or some useful objects. And then they would move on.

The family photos showed that Leo's father had always been an acrobat, like his grandfather and his uncles. Leo's mother had come to this country as a baby. She and his father had met at a gathering of the first arrivals, and they'd married.

Leo was calmer now. Maybe he would wait a while longer, wait until they got worried, until they called him, looked for him, maybe even apologized. After that he'd get back on board, victorious, proud, cleansed, avenged for the injustices he'd suffered. . . .

Leo was cold. He opened his eyes and lay still for a moment, trying to get his bearings. Outside. He had slept outside. Leo raised his head. The sun had come up and . . . and . . . the houseboat had disappeared! Left without him. How could they have left without him? *How?* Hadn't they seen that his bed was still made, that it hadn't been slept in? His father must have weighed anchor at dawn, as he sometimes did, while everyone was still asleep. They had vanished.

"They can't be far away. I'll wait for them, I won't move, they'll come back for me, they won't leave me here, they can't do that, they can't do that to me."

All day long Leo stayed by the edge of the stream, not daring to move for fear of missing them.

CHAPTER 2

Waiting

While he watched the stream, Leo noticed that the current was strong. The houseboat followed the current. Would it be able to turn and come back upstream once his family noticed he was missing? He became more and more worried as time passed, panicking, until his fear grew into a huge black hole filled with uncertainty. And Leo was terribly cold.

The early-morning sounds of this new day in the heart of the forest did not change his feeling of loneliness. And this loneliness was nothing like the loneliness he felt when the others made fun of him. Even when he was angry at them, he was still with his family. Leo was truly alone now, in an environment that was strange, maybe even hostile. On days when they were performing, he and his family would often leave the houseboat and walk around the edge of the forest. But Leo didn't know how to look for food, how to protect himself from the cold — how to deal with dangers. What kind of dangers *were* there here on land?

"I won't move, I won't move, I'll wait for them . . ."

He imagined that they would drop anchor, then start out on a path in the forest as soon as someone realized that he wasn't on board. . . . But his anxiety persisted. Maybe they wouldn't come looking for him. Maybe they'd left him there on

purpose — abandoned! Abandoned . . .
no, that was impossible. Yet his father was
always saying:

"What am I going to do with you? You'll
never amount to anything."

Leo had heard people talk about "too
many mouths to feed." His heart pounded
in his chest; he could hear it beating in his
ears. He was shaking, out of breath. His
mind was made up: he wouldn't budge.
That was one of the rules he'd been taught
if ever he was lost. He was afraid of strange
animals and he was hungry.

"I may be lame, but I'm an acrobat. I'll
climb a tree and wait patiently till they
arrive. I'll watch for them."

In the big oak where Leo had taken shelter, there were lots and lots of acorns. At
least he wouldn't starve to death. After he
had eaten, he found a nice warm place to
nestle in — an abandoned birds' nest. The

birds had gone away, too. They'd left for warmer countries where they would be far from the cold. The nest was comfortable, all things considered, and exactly the right size for Leo. Once again, he could tell from the size of the tree and the dimensions of the nest just how small he was.

"I really haven't grown very much."
Seconds, minutes, finally hours passed. He was vigilant, hopeful. He examined his

surroundings. He listened for the slightest sound, watched for the slightest movement, hoping for something familiar: the shifting of a shadow, for instance, that would turn out to belong to someone he knew. He hadn't moved a hair all day long. It was bitterly cold now.

Leo needed his own warm house and a hot meal. His mother's mushroom soup would be marvellous right about now. He felt his lips start to quiver and he could no longer hold back his tears. He allowed himself to have a good cry.

The sun was setting on the horizon. The days were so short at this time of year. He couldn't stay up here in the nest all night. He must look for a better shelter. Though it was urgent for Leo to climb down and start searching, he kept putting it off. When he finally decided to descend and begin his search, his chances of being found had dropped like the sun behind the horizon.

His parents had abandoned him completely. One whole night, one whole day — and nothing. Surely his absence had been noticed by now. They knew, they had to know. Had they even tried to find him? They must have been glad to be rid of him. If that was so, Leo would act as if they'd never existed. He would be free of them, too.

Bursting with anger, with hurt, with rage, and sorrow, Leo set out in search of a place where he could stay. He filled the hood of his cape with acorns, put some in his bag as well, and in a strong voice, started singing a song to drive away wild animals — and his fear.

Leo had been walking for a while now. The night was pitch-black, the sky full of stars. He didn't know if he had gone in a straight line or in a circle. He no longer heard the sound of water.

"I must have moved away from the river."

Finally, in a huge tree that resembled the

big oak, he spotted a lantern above a little door half hidden by ivy. To Leo's surprise there was a number on it: the number *0*.

He was reassured. No very big animal could get through such a tiny door. That's what made him decide to knock. He took hold of the knocker and thumped it against the door.

Boom, boom, boom.

He waited for a long time.

CHAPTER 3

A Place to Stay

"Oh my goodness! Who goes there?"

"Leo Polatouche, High Wire Artist, sir."

"I'm coming, I'm coming. Just a minute. The very idea, making such a racket at this hour of the night!"

Finally, the door opened. Facing Leo was a mole wearing a dressing gown and night cap, thick slippers, and an enormous pair of glasses. On a band around his head, Mr. Mole wore a lantern to light his way.

"My name is Griffon and this is my

house. Stand in the light so I can see you better. What is it you want, child?"

"Shelter for the night, sir, if you please."

"Come, step inside, it's bitterly cold. Lucky for you that the lantern at the door was still lit!"

He was amazed by what he saw next. From this level tunnels led directly underground, into absolute darkness. The lantern on Mr. Griffon's forehead gave Leo a glimpse of the entrances. Only one that went in a straight line behind Mr. Mole was lit here and there with lanterns hanging from the walls. Another world. Leo had always lived on the water, or on its frozen surface during winter breaks. Never in a tree, never underground.

Everything was clean, smooth . . . but there was a smell . . . a strong smell that Leo didn't recognize.

"Follow me, I'm going to introduce you to Melody. Melody is my wife."

"What's that smell, Mr. Griffon?"

"Why, there's no smell at all! Now let's hurry, it's cold out."

Mr. Griffon shut the door securely and they started to go down. Leo was a little worried, even though he knew that moles don't eat flying squirrels, not even those that are very small and have a paw. . . . That paw was very sore now. Leo was limping. After a few hours' walking, his boot always chafed. Mr. Griffon had turned around to see if Leo was following.

"Are you hurt?"

"No, sir, I just have a sore paw."

"Here we are. Oh, Melo-o-o-dy, we have a young visitor, prepare some warmth."

To inform her, Mr. Griffon had shouted into the tunnel, his voice echoing. What a strange way he had of saying things! What did he mean, "prepare some warmth"? Leo felt somewhat reassured now that he had shelter, but he definitely wasn't going to let his guard down.

I have to stay vigilant, Leo thought. *I'm not going to let him soften me up like that. Prepare some warmth . . . prepare warmth . . . what if they're ogres!*

"It's coming, Griffon, it's coming, I'm preparing, I'm preparing."

Leo heard soft singing. The musty smell of damp earth was getting stronger and stronger, making him cough and sneeze.

"You must have caught a chill on this bitterly cold night."

"No, sir, I think it's the odour."

"What odour? I can't smell a thing."

Leo didn't say another word about the smell. Griffon's lantern only lit up the area ahead of them. Leo was walking in the mole's shadow. Griffon was big and hefty and he, Leo, looked as if he were walking between the legs of a faceless giant. Griffon took big, heavy steps, his arms swaying rhythmically, while Leo, whose steps were short and jerky, tried to keep up and not let this strange character who was in the lead get too far ahead of him.

Leo had started to tremble again, from fatigue and cold, from hunger and fear. Just as his tears were about to start flowing anew, the tunnel opened into a large lighted square that contained all sorts of objects, each one more peculiar than the other. Melody approached Leo. He held back his tears and bravely introduced himself.

"I'm Leo Polatouche, High Wire Artist."

"And I'm Ms. Melody, Mr. Griffon's wife. Welcome to our home. Was it the lantern at the door that brought you here?"

Ms. Melody was smaller than Mr. Griffon and she was chubby and round. She moved as heavily as her husband, and like him, she wore thick glasses.

"Hurry and take off that damp cape or you'll catch your death of cold."

Leo did as he was told. The acorns he had gathered fell out of his hood and onto the floor.

"Oh! You've brought us some acorns."

She wrapped a big blanket around him. It was so warm! As if she'd taken it straight out of an oven. Mr. Griffon spoke up.

"I think it's too late to prevent the cold; he already coughed in the tunnel. The youngster says that it's the odour. Tell me, Melody, can you smell anything?"

She sniffed for a long time.

"No, I can't smell a thing, he must be coming down with something."

But there had been a smell. Leo remembered how it leaped to his nose in the tunnel. At least here in this room, the smell was not so strong.

"Come up to the fire, Leo, I'll bring you something to eat. You must be hungry. I'll use the acorns you've brought to make you a delicious pie tomorrow."

The objects around him started to attract Leo's attention. There were magnifying glasses everywhere. Some were fastened to hinged shafts, some were placed on small, wheeled platforms that could be moved around, while others, fastened to the dining table and the small end tables next to the armchairs, swivelled. Farther away, another one hung from a large "something" he'd never seen before.

It was a strange object consisting of several reeds of different diameters and heights. At the base of each was a good-sized bellows and the whole thing was firmly bound together with woven cords. In front of it stood a little bench.

"What is that?"

"It's a forest harmonium. I'm very proud of it. It isn't quite finished yet, but even so, Melody can play and practise."

"Eat your soup, Leo Polatouche. We'll explain it all by and by," Melody added.

The soup was thick and hot, made from different grains and flavoured with rose-water. Leo didn't get to see the bottom of his bowl. He fell asleep somewhere between the middle and the end of his meal.

That night he had a horrible dream. He was in a huge black cavern, groping his way along, when he touched something spongy on the wall. He tried to free his paw but he couldn't. It sank in deeper. He pushed against the wall with his other paw to release himself, but that paw was also imprisoned by the wall. That wall, that spongy thing, was going to swallow him whole. He was going to be completely gobbled up. And the smell! That musty smell.

Leo cried out and woke up on the floor. He could hear steps on one of the staircases. Then he spied a small lantern carried by Ms. Melody. Leo was quaking with cold and fear. She approached him slowly, speaking very softly.

"Don't be frightened, Leo, it's me, Ms. Melody. You must have had a terrible nightmare. Go back to bed. I'll stay with you for a while. I'm going to sit on this chair. When you've gone back to sleep I'll leave you the night light. Go to sleep now. There's no danger here, you're safe. Nothing bad will happen to you."

Ms. Melody helped Leo climb back into his little bed and get into a sleeping bag that was as soft inside as the warm blanket she'd wrapped him in when he first arrived. He went back to sleep after he'd opened and closed his eyes several times to check that Ms. Melody was still there with the lantern.

Leo was wakened by sounds below him. The little lantern was still burning. Leo's bed was in a recess in the wall, in an alcove. On a small bench next to it were laid some articles of heavy woven clothing: brown pants, green shirt with initials embroidered on it, long, thick socks, and laced, leather-soled slippers like the ones Mr. Griffon and Ms. Melody wore.

Leo got dressed. In the light of the lamp he noticed a spiral staircase to his right, and in front of him, a big, carved wooden screen that divided the room in two. Leo was curious. He stepped cautiously onto the first step. He realized as he went down that the staircase had been built inside a big tree root.

The staircase followed the natural curve of the enormous root. The banister was very smooth, the steps uneven. He walked carefully, with one hand holding the lantern and the other hand on the banister. When he emerged, Leo found himself in the big room he'd been in the night before.

CHAPTER 4

Disaster

They were both at the table. Mr. Griffon was reading his newspaper with a magnifying glass and Ms. Melody was eating — also with a magnifying glass. There was an empty bowl between them. All the lamps were lit, but it was still very dark in the room. Shyly, Leo approached the table. Griffon looked up at him and gave him a little nod.

"Good morning, little Leo. Look, Melody, the clothes are a good fit."

Though Leo hated being called little, he

returned the greeting. Melody quickly got up and filled the empty bowl.

"Sit down, Leo. Did your bad dream go away?"

"Yes, it did, Ms. Melody."

She brought the bowl and moved one of the magnifying glasses to put over it.

"Oh dear, I forgot, you certainly don't need this. But maybe I could do something for your paw."

"Why is it so dark in your house?" Leo asked.

"Because we live in the heart of this old tree that's been in our family for generations and generations. Look at the staircase, the one you came down. Everyone who has lived here has carved our family history in it. It's a family tree," Griffon explained.

Melody told him that the names of all the members of the mole families who had lived there — parents, grandparents, great-grandparents, and children — were written there. Then she asked him the last question he wanted to hear.

"What were you doing out in the cold, all by yourself, without your family?"

Leo kept eating, head down over his bowl, for a few seconds. What should he say? He didn't want to talk about his anger, or to explain that he'd run away to punish his family, or to confess that he'd been caught at his own game and that things had got out of control, and he was in much too deep. No. He would tell them instead a story that wouldn't cause him to lose face. He didn't want to risk being thrown out of this house because of his running away or his thoughts of revenge. They were bound to think that he'd misbehaved terribly. So he only confessed a small part of the truth.

He told them that when the show was over, everyone had gone to bed, but that he hadn't felt sleepy. It had been their last performance before winter. He'd left the houseboat without making a sound so he wouldn't disturb anyone. Without realizing it, he had fallen asleep at the foot of the big oak, a few steps from shore. His parents hadn't noticed his absence. When he woke up in the morning, the houseboat was gone. Piling on the details, Leo talked about waiting in the nest of a migratory bird at the top of the big oak, and about trying to find a shelter. And that was it.

Melody and Griffon exchanged a look in silence — an uncomfortable silence. Leo was struck with panic again. They hadn't believed his story. They were going to call him a liar and kick him out.

"Look, child," said Griffon finally. "The Magpie arrived with this morning's paper. The last one of the season, as a matter of fact. There's a story in it that we're going to read to you. It's very important. Something has happened."

Using the big magnifying glass, Griffon

slowly read the story in a low voice to Leo.

"A houseboat with the Polatouche family on board ran aground late yesterday morning. Extremely strong currents or a bad manoeuvre by the captain might explain this unfortunate accident. At this time there is no information about the inhabitants of the floating house. It is hoped that they have found shelter on the outskirts of the forest. The search will continue until freeze-up."

Griffon moved the magnifying glass and folded the paper; in silence, Melody looked at Leo. It was very cold again. Leo started to shiver and tears began to fall onto his cheeks. He was sure that it was all his fault. He knew that his father was a good sailor; he never made an error. It was because of Leo's escapade that this catastrophe had happened. They were all dead because of him.

That same day Leo took sick. Very sick. The moles carried him to bed. He was like a

marionette without strings. His brain could no longer control his legs or his arms or his hands. He stayed for a long time in his little bed in what seemed to be a permanent fog.

He could hear, as if from very far away, Mr. Griffon approaching his bed, staying for a while, then going to the other side of the screen on the left of the alcove. Then Ms. Melody appeared in the dense fog. She sat beside his bed in the big armchair where she'd sat when he had the nightmare. The lanterns were lit and she knitted, embroidered, or read through the magnifying glass fastened to the armrest. Leo had the vague impression that now and then Ms. Melody was humming. She also brought him hot broth and helped him drink it. Sometimes he felt himself being carried in someone's arms. They were Mr. Griffon's: they changed his clothes, remade his bed, put something warm deep inside his soft sleeping bag.

One day he felt a cold draft. He heard

voices behind the screen. A door shut. He opened his eyes and saw a stranger approach his bed. There were three in his room: Mr. Griffon, Ms. Melody, and this stranger all covered in grey. Ms. Melody spoke softly to him.

"We've asked the doctor to come and examine you. It won't hurt, but he will have to touch you."

Leo opened his eyes wider and saw an ermine, still in his autumn garb. He was wearing a mask. Leo was terribly frightened. Everyone knows that ermines are carnivores. It wasn't a mask, it was probably a muzzle. He was going to be a meal for an ermine! Probably Griffon and Melody were going to sell him.

"Don't be frightened, I'm not going to eat you! Ha! Ha! Ha! I'm afraid we ermines have a very bad reputation. Now, let me examine you."

Leo, helpless to react, let the ermine pat

him, palpate him, listen to his lungs with a stethoscope. The doctor also looked at his paw and said, "Hmm!"

After that, the three of them withdrew behind the screen. Again, Leo felt the cold air from outside, then Mr. Griffon and Ms. Melody reappeared. And then nothing — except the fog in his head.

Later, Leo would learn how many days he had spent in that comatose state, barely conscious and so very weak. But one morning he woke to find the fog had finally lifted. He felt as if he'd run backwards down a very, very long road, and that he was now back in the moles' house; fallen into a big black hole and now was climbing out. He still missed his family, but he wanted to get up and go to Mr. Griffon and Ms. Melody. Leo was very weak. His paws were as limp as cattail cotton.

Leo went down the family-tree staircase. With one hand he grasped the smooth banister for support. With the other, he held the little lamp that he'd found by his bed. Downstairs, all was quiet. Only a few lanterns lit the room. Mr. Griffon was feeding logs to the fireplace and poking the fire.

"Is that you, little one?"

"Yes, Mr. Griffon."

"Glad to see you up and about! Come and sit where it's warm. I always feed the fire in the morning before Melody sets foot on the floor. Her feet are always freezing. She likes the house to be cozy. I don't know another creature who's as sensitive to the cold as she is. That's why there are blankets warming above the fireplace."

They were both whispering.

"Anything new this morning?"

It was Melody's voice. It came from behind a colourful, heavy woven curtain. Leo had never noticed their bedroom, a room in back of the fireplace. He realized that he didn't know a thing about this house: he had sensations, impressions — that was all. The heavy fireplace was two-thirds of the way up the big gallery, and the stove for cooking food was a few steps away. You had to go around the fireplace to gain access to the moles' bedroom.

"I made some warmth, Melody," said Mr. Griffon, his voice stronger now, but still soft.

Leo felt that there was, in the atmosphere of this house, something extremely gentle, but at the same time painful. He didn't know if he should breathe deeply or listen to the tremendous sadness that swept over him when those two spoke to one another. Things seemed to unfold at a different rhythm, in a different time. Leo had no reference points. Nothing resembled anything he'd known before. What came closest was the winter lull, the unavoidable stop, the houseboat moored at the end of a stream. The period when there was no activity or concern.

Ms. Melody came out from behind the heavy curtain. She had on a loose bathrobe made from the same cloth that had warmed Leo so well when he first arrived. She had put on her thick slippers, her glasses of course, and she'd tied a bonnet under her chin.

"Good morning, Leo. I see you've decided to join us. *Brrr.* I'll never get used to this cold, it cuts through me to the marrow of my bones."

She touched Mr. Griffon's arm, her way of saying good morning just to him. And at the same time, it was a kind of thank-you. After that she bustled about and Mr. Griffon stopped moving.

"Today I'm going to make a pie with the acorns you brought, Leo. I've kept them. You have to get your strength back gradually. I don't want you running all over the place. You'll take one step more every day. We'll test the waters."

Already, Leo was tired. He'd stopped listening but some words were floating in his head: "test the waters." That reminded him of the houseboat. And that reminded him that even though he'd fallen from the high wire, he was Leo Polatouche the Acrobat. Which was something he must never forget.

That morning Ms. Melody served them pancakes with honey. Absolutely delicious. Then Leo had an amazing experience. After breakfast, Melody went to the strange object called the forest harmonium. With a large magnifying glass adjusted above her hands, she began to play. All Leo's hair stood on end. The music tickled him. He started to breathe, to breathe deeply. In the notes he heard sounds from life outside: wind, all sorts of winds, birds, all types of birds, rain.

And then all the memories of every landscape he had ever seen came alive in the
deep darkness: streams, clouds, skies, the
daylight and the moonlight, all the smells,
the seasons. Everything.

"When you feel strong enough, child,
I'll show you around our house. There's
so much to discover. You'll be with us at
least until spring. After that, we'll see. In
the meantime, there's lots to do and lots to
learn."

"Yes, Mr. Griffon."

"Griffon, give him some time."

They weren't going to make him leave.
They were offering him a roof over his
head, some unknown things to discover, a
new life. But this time it was for real. This
time it wasn't some adventure that he and
his brothers and sisters had made up. Here,
aside from the clothes he was wearing when
he arrived, his bag, and his woollen cape,

nothing was left of his "before." Not even the slightest trace. For now, he would have to drop anchor here. Grandfather and his boat language inhabited him still.

CHAPTER 5

The New House

Griffon led Leo to the forest harmonium. To the right of the instrument a wide, woven curtain hung on the wall. Griffon pushed it aside to reveal a door with a big number *1* carved into it. Griffon had pulled up the same big magnifying glass on wheels that Melody used to see the keys of the harmonium and pushed open the door. He retraced his steps, left the magnifying glass, and decided instead to tie a smaller one around his forehead.

"I forgot, you don't need one."

He picked up a lantern and asked Leo to follow him inside.

The deep, dense darkness surrounded Leo. The memory of his nightmare came back. But the ground here was firm and flat, the walls solid. Leo wasn't about to be swallowed alive. With his eyes he followed the halo of light that encircled Griffon as he moved.

"Stay still, child, I'm making light."

Leo felt as if he were shrinking when Griffon stepped away from him. On the opposite wall a lantern had just been lit.

"Phew!"

As Griffon walked, he counted his footsteps out loud: the number of steps determined the distance between lamps: "One, two, three, four," and a few seconds later, another lantern would light up. Now Leo could see the room.

"There you go, this is our storeroom. A real hodgepodge."

Leo imagined that this shambles must resemble the hold of the ship on which his grandfather, along with his family and other immigrants, had made the crossing. Leo walked toward Griffon. It was colder in this room, but the air was scented.

"Mmm!" said Leo. "It smells good."

"That's the seeds and dried flowers Melody has collected for making her oils and spices."

Along the wall there were shelves of transparent glass jars. They held wild fruit preserves — cherry, blackberry, raspberry, strawberry; rose petal jelly; honey. Hanging from woven straps were sprigs of rosemary, and poppies, and thyme. On the floor were piled-up bags of different flours: wheat, buckwheat, corn, rye. Griffon stated the name of each and pointed it out to Leo. He also showed him the bundles of hemp used to make clothing; straw for beds; silk from milkweed pods for pillows and for padding warm clothes. There was also a stock of exotic woods for carving and for making furniture: blocks, planks, branches, reeds of every size. Leo followed Griffon step by step. Together, they toured the storeroom.

In the hold of the houseboat there was stock for the winter, but it was nothing like this well organized mess. What Leo liked most in this black cave was the perfume in the air. When they finally left, the air in the main gallery made him sneeze again.

"Have you still got that cold?"

"I don't think so, Mr. Griffon."

"Melody, we have to find a stronger remedy for the youngster. Listen to him. He still has a cold!"

Ms. Melody raised her head to look very closely at Leo. "Don't fuss, Griffon. I think he's doing quite well." She was standing at the table, hard at work. Her hands were white with flour; a wooden rolling pin lay next to a ball of dough.

"I boiled up the acorns you brought from the forest, Leo. Now I have to slice them very fine and add them to a mixture of honey and rosewater."

That was how she made her acorn pie.

"Griffon, I'm out of water and the bottle is empty. Will you go and fetch me some? I'd like to straighten out some more pie crusts."

Another of their weird expressions, thought Leo. *Straighten out some pie crusts.* The words only added to his feeling of strangeness.

"We'll go now. Come along, child, I'll show you. And then I'll take you around the workshop."

Beneath the stairs, a big wooden barrel sat on a tall wheeled structure. The barrel was equipped with a small, attractively carved tap. Mr. Griffon rolled it out and pushed it toward the tunnel of door *0* — the one through which Leo had arrived. Griffon offered him a lantern, but Leo didn't take it.

I'm sure he's taking me to the exit, Leo thought. "I'd rather stay here, please," he said.

"As you wish, child, as you wish. I wonder, are you still afraid?"

The remark hurt Leo as if a thorn had been stuck into his skin. He wasn't going to let Mr. Griffon call him a coward. It was too much like what went on in the past when he refused to climb up to the highest wires. Not from fear. It was because he was certain that, once again, he was going to fall. This Mr. Griffon was going to see that Leo wasn't a worrywart or a crybaby or a foot-dragger. Leo picked up the lantern.

Climbing a little way up the sloping tunnel, they turned onto a fork that Leo hadn't noticed on the night when he'd arrived at the moles' house. From there he could hear the sound of water, of running water. Water, here? It had the same effect on him as the forest harmonium. Leo started breathing more easily. There was an underground spring! The feeling of suffocation vanished; his lungs opened. He felt happy — joyful, and all the tension in his body relaxed. The sound of water grew louder. Holding his lantern, Leo started to walk very fast, almost running. At last, something that he knew, that he loved, that bore some resemblance to his life.

Griffon moved to the right and Leo saw water flowing in a small channel. A water pitcher, surmounted by a big magnifying glass, hung from a root that stuck out of the clay wall. There were certainly a lot of magnifying glasses everywhere. Griffon lit another lantern near where the water came out.

"You are a Polatouche, an acrobat, and since you're here, do you think you could clean that magnifying glass? My eyesight isn't very good and I'd need another glass to clean it. Ha, ha! And I'd have to climb up there, and climbing is something I'm not too good at!"

"Yes, Mr. Griffon, I can do it."

"I'll fill this pitcher for you. Climb up to the magnifying glass. When you're up there, I'll pass you the pitcher. Empty the water onto it, to wash it. Understand?"

"Yes."

And Leo, even though his paws were

still weak, climbed nimbly onto the structure supporting the lens and waited.

"You're there? Already? You're hired. As of now you're our household's lens-polisher. I can't wait to tell Melody. It's a terrible problem for us."

For Leo, this news was both good and bad. It meant that they weren't going to send him away — but it also meant that he wouldn't be seeing his parents for a while.

And what if the story in the newspaper was a lie? Leo didn't know how to read very well. He could recognize numbers and letters, but he couldn't read easily yet. Maybe he was simply being held a prisoner here. Victim of an ambush, a frame-up. Leo decided that he ought to draw up an escape plan. But then he remembered how kind the moles were; he remembered the warm clothes, the way they'd cared for him, fed him. It was he who had come to them. All these thoughts raced crazily around in his head as he cleaned, handed the pitcher back to Mr. Griffon, and climbed down to stand beside him.

"Where does this water go, Mr. Griffon, and where does it come from?"

"There are all kinds of underground springs, Leo. They're a little like the veins in your body or the pathways in the forest. The doctor explained it to me. At a certain point, they join up to form streams and rivers. Your family followed those streams and rivers. It's all the same water."

Leo didn't ask any more questions, but he wondered how it was that there was always water that didn't stop flowing. Mr. Griffon hadn't answered his question. Did the water go all the way around the earth? Maybe Grandpa could have told him. Leo dipped his nose in the water and drank.

Brrrrr! It was cold! He even dipped his paws into the little pool that formed at the foot of the spring. His sleeves were soaking wet. Meanwhile, Mr. Griffon calmly filled his water barrel.

Silently, they returned to the tunnel that would take them home. Mr. Griffon didn't have to exert himself too much. The floor sloped gently down to the main tunnel so the barrel rolled along easily on its platform. Leo took tiny steps ahead of Mr. Griffon. This time, he was the one who lit their way. He held up the lantern at arm's length. The light formed a little circle around them. The sound of trickling water faded as they advanced, but in the silence Leo was able to keep it alive in his ears. There was still the *slip-slop* of water in the barrel.

"How do you expect me to take care of your cold if you let your fur and your clothes get wet like that! Come here and get into something dry this minute, Leo Polatouche."

Ms. Melody was in a terrible mood. The table had been tidied, the acorn pie was ready to go into the oven. Taking Leo by the hand, she led him to the big fireplace. She reached up and took down a towel that was clean but rough, and another shirt. Both towel and shirt were warm.

"Now take off those wet things."

Vigorously, she rubbed Leo's paws. It warmed him. He put on the dry shirt. She hung the wet one from the magnifying glass next to Mr. Griffon's chair.

"You know, Melody, the youngster is very good at cleaning lenses. He could be a real help in the house."

"Don't try to soften me up with your little schemes . . ." She was in a really terrible mood. ". . . Can you really wash the magnifying glasses? It's so hard for us!"

She seemed to be softening so Leo ventured to speak.

"It's true, Ms. Melody. I cleaned the one at the fountain. I could show you if you like. Climbing is easy for me."

He was proud that he could say he knew how to climb and no one here would compare him to someone else who was better. Here, he was the best climber.

During his wife's little temper flare-up, Mr. Griffon had stowed his water barrel under the stairs. He stirred up the stove and fed it a few more logs. Then he put the biggest logs into the fireplace. He settled comfortably into his chair, but didn't stay there. He couldn't read his book because Leo's shirt, which was draped over his magnifying glass, got in the way. Sighing, but without a word to Ms. Melody, he took the shirt and hung it over another lens, the one on the forest harmonium. Apparently, he didn't want to risk any more trouble with Ms. Melody in such a mood.

Chapter 6

What a Strange Way to Live!

Leo had no idea of the time or the day or even of where he was. He had no reference point. The only light came from the lamps. In this perpetual gloom, activities changed, they ate and slept, but they seemed always to be in the same minute.

When he was living outdoors there was always day and night. Leo could even identify some of the constellations in the sky. Grandpa had taught him how to distinguish those of summer and those of winter. He had even seen the northern lights. He could tell from which direction the wind blew by the way the tree branches moved on shore. From the path of the sun, he could tell if it was morning or noon or the end of the day. Here, there was nothing but night — black, black night — and the smell that made him cough.

"What day is it?"

The question had come out just like that, without warning. Mr. Griffon and Ms. Melody looked at one another for a moment. At first they didn't say anything.

"Griffon, you could turn over the hour-glass. I'm going to put this pie in the oven. It will be ready in time for our meal."

Mr. Griffon got up and reached for something on the mantelpiece next to many other similar objects that were bigger or smaller. He upended the third in a long series.

"This one, child, counts the hours. Melody bakes her pie for one hour. In this one, it takes six hours for the sand to run out. And this one, twenty-four hours. The one between them — twelve. And here are the smallest ones, for the minutes. It's a simple system but it took me a long time to perfect. I had to find the right kind of sand — fine or coarse — and then make openings of the right size. The only thing is, you mustn't forget to turn over the hourglass at the end of the day."

The timepieces were made of magnifying glass. *You really have to look at everything through a magnifying glass in this land of the near-sighted*, Leo thought.

"How do you keep track of what day it is?"

"You think of everything, Leo Polatouche. Look at my apron," said Melody. Her bad mood had lifted.

Patiently, she showed him two pieces of cloth pinned to the little pockets on her apron. On one was embroidered *Monday*. On the other, a little snow scene.

"Wait," she said.

She shuffled toward the bedroom, then disappeared behind the heavy curtain. A few minutes later, she came out carrying a small wooden box. Leo was sitting on a thick rug next to the big fireplace. She set down the box beside him and opened it. It contained an astounding number of little pieces of embroidered cloth illustrating natural phenomena: wind, rain, snow, sun, flowering trees, high grass, fruit, and so forth, along with the days of the week.

"You'll see! I think you'll get used to our codes. We had to find a way to keep track of time up above during the winter."

"What's on the bib of your apron, Ms. Melody?"

Embroidered on the top of the apron was a number, preceded by a plus and a minus sign.

"That? It's the date."

"But why the plus sign and the minus sign?"

"That's for chance," said Griffon. "It helps us know more or less what day it is. Melody changes her apron every morning. It's as good as turning the pages of a calendar. She adds the embroidery. Melody's apron is both our calendar and our weather forecast. We like to be precise."

What a strange world! Leo thought. *It's very precise, but everything in it seems vague. When I look through their lenses everything is hazy, but to them, things are clearer.* "So that means today is November 23? How many days have I been here?"

"You're starting your eighth day, Leo dear. You've been very sick. So sick that Doctor Ermine came. He very rarely pays house calls."

At that moment and without warning, a turmoil of despair, sadness, and rage was set loose in Leo's stomach. He started to cry, softly at first, then more loudly. Before long, he was screaming.

"Eight days! I want out. I'm not sick anymore. I want to leave here right now! I want to see my parents again, I don't want to live underground. I'm not like you and I don't *want* to be like you. You haven't got the right to keep me prisoner. I'm not your slave. You took everything away from me, I haven't got anything from my family, nothing to remember them by. I haven't even got my own clothes. . . . Besides, it smells bad here. . . . It stinks! It smells like rotten old mushrooms!"

Griffon and Melody stayed in their chairs, one on either side of the hearth; silently, they waited for Leo's angry cries and his terrible pain to subside. He sat on the floor between them, on the comfortable rug that Melody had woven. He was sobbing as if his life were over.

All the sand in the hourglass for the acorn pie had now run out. Melody got up to take the pie from the oven. When she

59

came back, she draped the woollen cape over Leo's shoulders, which comforted him a little. Very calmly, Griffon spoke.

"We are offering you hospitality. It's winter, there's snow out there now. It's part of our way of living to open our door to those in need. You're free to stay, or to go. About your parents, I hope that they're safe and warm like you. In the spring we'll certainly hear something about them and the floating house. As for memories, if you want, we'll do something to keep them alive. Melody and I have ways to do that. And don't be afraid of Doctor Ermine. He's a vegetarian. We'll talk about your paw later on. Now child, calm down."

"Do you want to show him right away, Griffon?"

"Yes, Melody, I think the time has come, even though it's not finished."

Mr. Griffon got up, took a lamp, and went in the opposite direction to the storeroom to the place he called the workshop. Leo hadn't been there yet. Griffon came back holding a piece of cardboard covered with a cloth. He put it down beside Leo, who stopped crying. He was intrigued. His anger had melted away

"Now blow your nose, Leo."

He did, then gently lifted the cloth that concealed a sheet of paper. Before his eyes was a picture of his whole family, himself included. He was speechless, flabbergasted. He touched the face of each member of his family. They were all there, in their costumes. The colours were a little different, but they were his people; it was his world.

"Where did this come from?"

"We may live underground, Leo Polatouche, but I'll have you know that Mr. Griffon wields a pencil better than anyone around. He receives all the newspapers, all the posters. On top of that, he's the census-taker for this part of the forest: he keeps track of births, deaths, and moves. Mr. Griffon's office is up above, behind the screen next to your bed."

"Is this for me, Mr. Griffon?"

"Yes it is, child. I still have to touch it up here and there. You can help if you want. We got this poster a few days before your show. I do this for every event that's a little bit special. I keep all the new ones in big note-books up above. I'm like a memory box."

"You put that very well," observed Melody.

It was time to eat. Leo kept the cape on while he helped Ms. Melody set the table. He learned where different household objects — cooking implements, bowls, plates — were stored. He had his very own place at the table, too: there was no magnifying glass and his back was to the hearth. He was between Griffon and Melody, with Melody next to the stove and Griffon across from her, on Leo's right. Under the circumstances, it was the right arrangement. They ate millet cakes and for dessert, Melody served the pie she'd made from the acorns that Leo had brought in his hood.

"Could I sleep down here with you?"

"Why not, eh, Melody? You can't sleep in our room, but I'll fix up something for you in a corner by the fireplace. You'll be warmer there than up above."

"We must have something in the workshop that will make him a comfortable bed, Griffon, don't you think?"

"We'll have a look after we've eaten. For now, youngster, eat."

"And the portrait, may I hang it beside my bed?"

"Why not, Leo? Griffon will find a way to put it up."

"When you're all better, child, we'll talk about your memories. It will be like opening Melody's wooden boxes. I'm sure we'll find all sorts of things."

"I've just got three or four little things. I don't have any others, Mr. Griffon."

"You've got some inside you. You'll see, it's not so hard. You might even learn how to turn them into pictures. Music helps with memories. Melody can show you how to play the forest harmonium. Now eat, eat."

Leo was feeling better. The moles weren't going to force him to turn away from his former life. But he had a heavy secret to drag around. And what if Griffon and Melody were to discover the tragedy he had caused? What if they found out that he was responsible for the death of his family? He would definitely be judged, punished, maybe even condemned to death. He'd hoped for an accident and it had happened. His grandfather had used an expression that terrified him when he talked about the laws of nature: "An eye for an eye, a tooth for a tooth — a life for a life." If the moles found out, it might be the end of Leo.

"Eat, Leo, before it's ice cold."

After they had eaten, Mr. Griffon and

Leo went to the workshop. To Leo's relief, the moles seemed to have forgotten the terrible harsh words he'd flung at them.

Against all expectations, a little bit of light filtered into this room, and it had nothing to do with lanterns. Above their heads, a small glass ceiling let in some daylight. Leo thought it was a very pretty place. Warm, too.

In the workshop there was another stove. A squat little stove, smaller than the one used for cooking, with a door in front for feeding the fire. On it sat a pot full of water with fragrant chips of wood floating in it.

"Those are cedar chips," said Mr. Griffon, who had followed Leo.

This room, smaller than the main gallery or the storeroom, was filled with a big workbench and a whole set of tools: clamps, planes, bit braces, hammers, wooden dowels, wood chisels, handsaws, and so on.

"Not bad, eh, youngster?"

"Oh, yes, Mr. Griffon! You've really got a lot!"

All at once he felt very poor. Neither his father nor his grandfather had ever owned so many things in their whole lives. They really had nothing. But Leo possessed riches that he didn't even know he had: the grandeur of all the landscapes he had seen, and the beauty of his travels on board the floating house. Inside him there were wonderful images, fantastic memories, unforgettable encounters with so many different creatures. Leo and his family had experienced what few others had known.

In the workshop too, there were many magnifying glasses, all covered with a thin coating of wood dust. Dusting those lenses would be a big job for Leo. Mr. Griffon was at the back of the workshop. From there he picked out a wicker basket.

"This should do the trick. We're going to fix you up a nice, comfortable bed. If we cut out this side of the basket, it will be easy for you to get in and out, and you'll be cozy and warm. Let's go show Melody. Melo-o-o-dy, look what I've come up with!"

"That's good, very good, I'll give you a hand," she said.

"I can help you, Mr. Griffon."

"Don't bother, Melody, the youngster will give me a hand. Take this side and wait for me. I'm going to put out the lanterns."

The only light now came from the lamp that Mr. Griffon wore around his forehead and the feeble daylight that came from the skylight. Yes, definitely, Leo liked this room very much. Because of the light and also because of the way it smelled.

Ms. Melody stood waiting for them at the door between the workshop and the gallery, hands folded on her apron. She had put away the remains of their meal and cleared the table.

"There you go, this will do the trick. I'll make you a comfortable mattress. I think we should put the basket there."

"Not so fast, Melody, I have to cut away a section on this side. That will make it easier."

"Come along, Leo. We're going to the storeroom. That's where we keep the bales of straw. We'll pack some into a burlap bag. Bring a lantern. Meanwhile, Griffon will cut the side of the basket."

In this house everything took such a long time. For every task, lanterns and lenses had to be lit and adjusted. Inactivity would have been so much easier. Leo felt extremely tired. Still weak from his illness, the day had seemed very long to him, like a night that would never end.

With a lantern on her forehead, Ms. Melody knew exactly where to go. Leo followed her, carrying a second lamp. She pulled a small cart along for transporting the material. She picked up a large bundle of straw, then looked for an empty sack. The two of them returned to the main gallery. While he was helping Ms. Melody fill the sack, Leo kept sneezing; the dry straw made him cough. Melody added some scented herbs to the straw.

"You haven't quite shaken off that cold yet. I'll give you some warm honey before you go to sleep."

One of the big hourglasses on the mantelpiece was almost empty. The day was ending. A very special day in the life of Leo Polatouche the Acrobat. Griffon and Melody finished making his new bed. Griffon even hung the poster on the wall next to it. Ms. Melody had gone down below to fetch the sleeping bag, the night light, and Leo's other clothes. The move was now complete.

Griffon and Melody went to their bedroom and came out a short time later. They had put on their nightclothes, the ones they'd been wearing the first time Leo had seen them. They sat down in their own armchairs near the hearth, Ms. Melody holding some embroidery work under a magnifying glass, Mr. Griffon with a wooden shelf covered in heavy paper, under a lens as well. He dipped the claw on his right paw into a bottle of ink that sat on the end table and drew some letters. Leo, dead tired, was already in bed. Thinking he was asleep, they spoke in low voices. Leo could hear them.

"Melody, does our house really smell of mouldy mushrooms?"

"Of course not, Griffon, it's his cold; he's still coughing; and his sadness makes him say all sorts of things."

That night, Leo had another dream. There was a crowd, a throng all around him, just like on one of their show days. Everything seemed happy, the people were clapping in time as they repeated a counting rhyme. They were laughing very hard. Leo started listening to what they were saying. The people were laughing . . . laughing at him. "One, two, three, four, Leo's paw is really sore, let's pull his tail . . . " All their hands came closer to pull his tail. He was terrified at the prospect of seeing it fall off. He woke up.

There was a night light beside his bed and another hung by the curtain that separated him from the moles' bedroom. In the hearth there were still some glowing embers. Melody and Griffon weren't there. Most likely they'd gone to bed, too. Such silence! At home the dark was filled with gentle sounds: wind, frogs, insects, night birds, the lapping water, the breathing of his brothers and sisters. Here there was a total absence of sound. Leo fell asleep again imagining all those familiar noises, the sounds of his life. His memories.

CHAPTER 7

Outside at Last

The next morning, Leo was wakened by Mr. Griffon.

"Good morning, child. Stay warm. There's a heavy snowfall coming and I can't wait. It will protect the house against the elements and it won't be so cold inside. Not much snow fell last night. But after breakfast we should get rid of what there is on the glass roof before more comes."

Griffon was speaking as if to himself, his voice hushed. Leo had drifted back to sleep, just as he was trying to understand why a house needed protecting. When he opened his eyes again, Ms. Melody was up and dressed.

She had on a fresh apron: a new date and different embroidery. Little grey clouds above a snow scene on one pocket; on the other, the word *Tuesday*.

Leo wished he had been awake for their morning exchange of greetings. He would have liked to see Ms. Melody touch Mr. Griffon's arm as she'd done on the previous morning, saying *good morning* and *thank you* at the same time.

"Good morning, Leo Polatouche. Hurry and get dressed and make your bed. We're going to sit down and eat. We have plenty to do today."

Mr. Griffon had turned over a lot of hourglasses! The six o'clock one or the twelve o'clock? Leo didn't know. He didn't understand the system yet. It was still a mystery to him.

The meal was very much like the one of the day before. A bowl of grains boiled up together and sweetened with honey. Leo liked that mixture. When they were finished, Mr. Griffon gave him a piece of good news.

"Put on your warm clothes, youngster, we're going out!"

"Going out! I'll be ready in a minute."

Leo put on his cape, but then Ms. Melody put in her two cents' worth. She thought he wasn't dressed warmly enough. This led to a search in a trunk, which became very complicated.

Ms. Melody took out all kinds of heavy clothes. She held them at arm's length and studied them, passing her eyes over them in the dim light. She had Leo try them on and she set aside those that fit: wool-lined jackets, felt boots, mittens, toques, scarves. The clothes had the wonderful smell of cedar.

It took time, too much time for Leo's

liking. He was impatient to be outside. But Ms. Melody wouldn't let him go out in the cold dressed as he was. So Leo tried on the clothes, one garment after the other. On one side was a pile of spare outer clothes, on the other were the garments she would put back in the trunk.

"That's one good thing done. Now off you go! There's no risk that you'll be cold."

Finally, Mr. Griffon and Leo started up the family tree staircase. Leo followed Mr. Griffon, who was holding the lantern — and some tinted magnifying glasses. Leo held onto the banister. He was a little self-conscious in his new clothes.

They passed the alcove of his old bedroom, then they went behind the screen. Leo didn't have time to study the room. Maybe on the way back.

Griffon walked directly to a door and blew out the lantern. They wouldn't need it

now. The cold air came rushing in when he opened the door.

What a contrast! Outside, there was daylight. And despite the greyness, the light shone brightly on the snow. The weather forecast on Ms. Melody's apron was correct. For a brief moment Leo had to squint.

What joy! Fresh air! In just a few days the landscape had been totally transformed. The trees were now bare, except for some oaks that still had dry, brown leaves that shuddered in the wind — and there was the snow.

"Are you cold, child?"

"Oh no, Mr. Griffon. In fact, I'm hot. I'd like to take off my hat for a while."

"As you wish, child. Just don't let your ears freeze."

At last Leo could see the moles' house. There, before his eyes, was an old tree stump. The one with the staircase built inside it. He saw the door through which Doctor Ermine had entered when he'd come that night.

"Which door did I come through, Mr. Griffon?"

"Come over here, child, I'll show you. At the same time we can take the snow off the roof of the workshop. Then we'll be able to work in daylight."

They went around the stump and walked a short distance side by side. Griffon pointed to a big, bare tree. You could no longer see the door. The wind had come up and it was now hidden by a snowdrift.

"That's where you came in. Now let's go take a look at the roof."

The lantern that had guided him on the night he'd arrived had been taken down. Leo put his toque back on. It was very, very cold. These precious minutes were making him happy. *Stretch out time. Don't go back down right away. Stay outside.*

Down below he had the impression that he was dying a little, going out like the flame in a lantern. And those bad dreams! When he got his strength back he would be able to climb trees again, to work out when it wasn't too cold. And when his parents came to get him, he wouldn't have lost his abilities. That was what Leo Polatouche, the Acrobat, told himself as he walked along beside Mr. Griffon. Out here were sounds of life. He could hear birds. Even though he knew only a few, their songs were familiar. Mmm! Oh, it was all so good — the wind, the way things moved, the space.

He, who had lived most of his life on the water, now spent long hours underground like a mole, but without spectacles or magnifying glasses. By going outside every day he could also experience snow and severe cold.

When the houseboat was moored for the winter, the adults and the oldest children were always careful to put away whatever could not tolerate the freezing temperatures, and to fasten down whatever the wind might carry off. After that, the floating house was covered with evergreen boughs to keep the family as warm as possible. For the first few weeks, they were confined to the floor below deck. But then the branches dried, their needles dropped off, and the snow blanketed the fir boughs and enveloped the houseboat, keeping the family snug and warm. When the house resembled a mountain of snow, they could move back into the cabin on deck. They went there during the day. Below was the sleeping area. A space in the fore hold of the boat was used for storing food. The snow, thick or thin, that covered the portholes gave everything a milky tinge, creating a soft blur. Life was muted here. The sounds from outside, the variations in air and weather were muffled, deadened, when they were inside the houseboat. Only the cracking of the ice as it squeezed the walls of the houseboat disturbed them. Sometimes it sounded like a long lament.

Leo was thoroughly enjoying the playful breeze that brought scents and sounds along with it. High in the sky, clouds driven by a powerful wind created plays of bright light and shadow. Griffon and Leo walked in silence for a while, their breath creating small puffs of vapour. The thin layer of snow was dry and light. Walking was easy for Griffon, sheer delight for Leo.

He started to run. He wanted to get to the big blue spruce and climb it.

"Hey there, youngster, what are you doing?"

"Don't worry, Mr. Griffon, I just want to see the horizon."

In the tree, Leo tried to run from branch to branch, but his felt boots got in the way. Griffon stood at the foot of the big tree and waited.

"Are you all right there, child? What can you see?"

"I'm fine, Mr. Griffon. I think I can

see the stream. Is that possible? It looks frozen."

"Of course it's possible, we aren't very far from it. It serves as a thoroughfare, of water or ice, depending on the season. You'd better come down now. We have to go home, or Melody will be worried. We'll come back another day."

Leo was filled with hope and energy. As he climbed, he had dislodged colonies of blue jays and evening grosbeaks. They had taken flight in a group, forming a big circle in the sky around the tree, and now they'd come back to nest. Leo was so happy he could have cried.

On the ground again, walking next to Mr. Griffon, Leo dared to ask a question.

"Mr. Griffon, would you come out with me some night to see the stars? Even in the winter we used to go out with Grandpa to look at them. They're different from the ones you see in summer."

"I don't know anything about the stars, child. Besides, I can't see a single one, not even with my glasses. If you really want, though, I'll come out with you. Maybe Melody will agree to go outside for a while. We'll think about it. Now let's get moving. It's cold and we have work to do."

Although he didn't know it, Leo had just planted a desire in Mr. Griffon's inventive mind. With his skill at designing lenses for better vision, maybe he could invent a machine for looking at the stars with the youngster. They cleaned the snow off the glass roof of the workshop and went back inside.

Once again, Leo was struck by the contrast of shadow and light. When Mr. Griffon stepped inside the house, he lit a lantern. They took off their felt boots on the upper landing and went down to join Melody. She was playing the forest harmonium. Leo didn't take the time to question Mr. Griffon about this room, he'd save that for later.

There was time. When Ms. Melody heard them on the stairs, she stopped playing.

The rhythm of life had changed instantly and the musty smell was back. But in Leo's heart at that very moment, there was a little hourglass of well-being that was slowly measuring the time.

"You don't have to stop playing, Melody. I like listening to you, and so does Leo. I'm sure he does."

"Oh, I don't play well enough yet to give you a concert! I still need to practise. It will come. But that's enough for today. Did you have a good walk out there? It must be bitterly cold. Did you stay covered up, Leo, and you too, Griffon? I don't want you getting sick."

"It's very nice out, Ms. Melody. I even climbed up the big blue spruce, and I dislodged the evening grosbeaks and the blue jays. It was really fun. Have you got the sound of beating wings in the harmonium?"

"Goodness gracious! And you let him do that, Griffon?"

"You should have seen him, Melody. A real high wire artist. Even in felt boots."

Leo felt proud of himself, despite his imperfect paw.

"Yes, I think we have the sound of beating wings, don't we, Griffon? In fact if you want, I could show you, a little every day, how to create the sounds and make the harmonies. Would you like that?"

"Yes, Ms. Melody."

Leo Polatouche had not felt so good since the day of the disaster.

"I was going to fix a snack. You were out for a long time — are you hungry? I took out some cakes and the water's heating for herbal tea."

Mr. Griffon stood with his back to the fireplace, his hands behind him, warming up. Leo stood beside him and did the same. But he wasn't really cold, only happy. He raised his head and smiled up at Mr. Griffon. Mr. Griffon gave him a wink. Then Leo helped Ms. Melody put the bowls on the table and brought out the magnifying lenses.

CHAPTER 8

Leo's Talents

After their snack, they got down to work. Each of them had a task to perform. Mr. Griffon saw to the firewood, Ms. Melody sat at the loom, and Leo Polatouche got busy cleaning first the lenses in this room, then those in all the other rooms of the moles' house. It didn't matter if he didn't wash them all on the same day. Mr. Griffon was in charge of the hourglasses and the lamp oil.

Now, the day was drawing to an end. The last meal had been eaten and they were all

ready for sleep. Mr. Griffon and Ms. Melody were comfortably settled in their armchairs next to the fireplace. Using their magnifying glasses, he was writing, she embroidering. Leo was flat on his stomach on a cushion, stirring up the coals with a stick. When the end of it caught fire Leo blew on it to put it out.

"Ms. Melody, was it you who embroidered the initials on all the clothes I wear? Whose are they? There were two kinds in the big trunk."

Leo dared not ask the real question, the one that was nagging at him. He wanted to know if the moles had children and if so, where they were, what had happened to them. The answer didn't come right away. Leo had started playing with the coals again. Mr. Griffon explained.

"We have a grown son called Scribble. He's a geologist. He doesn't live with us anymore. They're his clothes that you're

wearing. Melody made them all. That's why we've got them in so many sizes."

"And as for the two kinds," Ms. Melody went on, "we also had a little girl named Dawn. She was very sick and couldn't get better. Doctor Ermine came to see her very often. Breathing was so hard for her that one day she stopped. That's all. . . . Their names are carved on the family tree staircase."

Ms. Melody's voice was deep and gentle, laden with memories.

"So you've lost somebody too?"

"That's right, Leo Polatouche, we have."

In the pause that followed, Leo searched for the right thing to say, but could only come up with, "I'm sorry." The moles nodded, lost for the moment in their memories. Leo waited for what seemed like a long time before he spoke again.

"Could I go outside again tomorrow?"

"Why not, child? Right now, though,

let's go to sleep. Shall I leave this lantern for you like I did the other night?"

"Yes, please, it's so dark here."

"Good night, Leo."

Ms. Melody had realized at once how happy it made Leo to be able to go outside and hear all the sounds of the forest. So, while Leo was getting into bed, she went to the harmonium and offered him the sounds of the wind and the rain and of running water. After that, every evening without fail, she played for Leo. Sometimes she combined sounds: the frogs with the wind, the owl's cry with the sound of water. She gave the wind a long, soft sound that lulled Leo, who quickly dropped off to sleep.

The days slipped by, all the same, all different. The date on Ms. Melody's aprons changed, along with the little embroidered scenes. The past weeks had been marked by nothing but snow, with or without sunshine.

A month went by. Leo continued to go out every day. He shovelled off the glass roof of the workshop, and while he was out, he climbed trees and played. A lot of snow had fallen. For his outings, Mr. Griffon had made him what he called *bears' paws* of woven sinew fastened to an oval wooden frame. Strips of burlap tied them to his felt boots. That way he didn't sink too deeply into the snow.

Leo learned how to play the forest harmonium. Ms. Melody taught him how he could press his paws onto the bellows that drove air into the reed-pipes, and what valves to pull to produce a short sound or a long one, and how to combine the sounds.

Two rows of pipes were fastened together and positioned by category: wind, water, birds. . . . Inside the pipes, Mr. Griffon had placed all kinds of small objects which, when driven by the air, moved to produce the desired sounds. For instance, the sound

of rain was created by using small hard seeds that clinked together inside the reed. To Leo it sounded exactly like rainy days in the floating house. Bits of dried leaves produced the windsong.

As for Mr. Griffon, he taught Leo how to handle tools. Leo was particularly fond of the wood chisels. Mr. Griffon had shown him how to fit little pieces of wood into the clamps and how to smooth wooden spoons. After that, Leo and Mr. Griffon polished them until they shone.

In the evening, after they'd eaten and before they went to bed, all were busy with something by the fire. Leo had almost finished making a wooden marionette. Mr. Griffon and Ms. Melody had helped him attach the strings and dress it.

Leo explored the room up above. It was where Mr. Griffon kept all his registers: the names of all the local inhabitants and where they lived. He saw the newspapers the

Magpie delivered during three of the four seasons. Leo paid close attention to Mr. Griffon when he used the big claw on his right paw to write. Ms. Melody sharpened it regularly and carefully. Griffon dipped that claw into the inkwell and, using a magnifying glass, delicately drew words. Over time, the claw had turned totally black. It wasn't dirty; it had been dyed by the ink.

That was how Leo learned to write, but using birds' feathers taken from empty nests. And most important, he learned how to draw. He liked tracing lines that brought alive his memories and illustrated everything around him now. He had a good sense of movement and of proportions. With a few strokes of the pen he could illustrate a setting and show an expression on a face. He created drawings to show the moles what his house looked like during the winter, both inside and out.

CHAPTER 9

Doctor Ermine Comes Back

One late-winter morning, nearly four months after Leo had come to live with the moles, someone knocked on the door of the room above. There stood Doctor Ermine. He had come to check on Leo, he said, but first he asked to speak to Mr. Griffon alone.

Leo, never completely comfortable in the presence of Doctor Ermine, was only too happy to give the pair their privacy. He went down to the kitchen to help Ms. Melody. While she made fruit cakes, Leo used a cookie cutter to shape some tea biscuits. They also made some of the unleavened rolls Leo was so fond of. The delicious aroma of their baking disguised the other unpleasant one. Leo had never quite gotten used to it after all this time.

The doctor and Mr. Griffon came down the stairs.

"Leo, child, Doctor Ermine would like to talk to you."

Leo was immediately worried.

"I'm fine now, Doctor, I'm not sick anymore."

Doctor Ermine was covered in white fur now. He didn't have on a mask or a muzzle. Leo may have dreamed that he was wearing them on the day of his first frightening visit. It was such a vague memory and such a big upheaval.

"Actually, it's because your health is so good now that I've come to see you. I was waiting till you felt better and had adapted to your new house. You do seem to be very well, indeed."

"Leo still coughs a little, Doctor, when he comes in from a walk. Is it wise for him to go running outside every day when it's so cold?"

"He'll be fine, Ms. Melody. I'm going to listen to your chest, Leo. Let's see. Pull up your shirt, I've brought my bag."

The doctor proceeded to examine Leo. He took his pulse, listened to his chest, looked at his throat, his ears, his eyes, struck his knees and elbows with a little hammer, and asked him to take off his boot. The doctor wanted to look at Leo's paw. In fact that was why he'd come. When the doctor ran his finger over the sole of Leo's paw, it tickled him and his toes contracted. The doctor seemed satisfied. He explained to Leo what he intended to do: he hoped to operate on his paw.

"Look, Leo. See how your toes are bound together by that web of skin? I'd like to cut it so that each toe is free. It would improve your balance. Then, at the back of your leg, right here, I'd like to make a small incision to make your tendon more elastic. Do you understand?"

"Does it mean I won't fall off the high wire anymore?"

"That, I can't guarantee. What I do know is that your paw would grow more normally, and as you get older, you wouldn't limp so much. You can think it over. I would prefer to operate on you now so that you have time to recover before spring and the break-up."

Leo's heart was pounding in his chest. He could hear it thudding in his ears.

"Will it hurt?"

"A little afterwards, maybe. We'll have Ms. Melody's help. She knows remedies that work very well. During the operation she'll give you a potion made from poppies, and I'll give you an injection, too. You won't feel any pain."

"We'll take good care of you, Leo. We think that you should have this operation. But we aren't your parents. Although if they were here I think that they'd agree."

Mr. Griffon shared Ms. Melody's opinion. Leo stalled for some time.

"What about the lenses and the glass roof and all the work?"

"Don't worry, child, we'll work out something. In any case, it won't be that long."

They finally decided that the operation would take place three days later, in Griffon and Melody's house. The doctor would perform the surgery in the workshop. Because of the glass roof, it had the best natural lighting. Leo would be able to lie on the workbench and it was warm there and it smelled good.

Leo couldn't stop thinking, *I'm going to have an operation, I'm going to have an operation. . . .*

Ms. Melody prepared bandages and made potions from her store of dried wildflowers and herbs. Meanwhile, in the workshop, Mr. Griffon fixed up a board on casters to which he fastened a solid chair with armrests. They could use it to move Leo across the rooms in the gallery without too much difficulty. With Ms. Melody, he also did a thorough housecleaning.

Leo took advantage of the three days to polish all the lenses in the house. He also spent long periods of time outside. After the doctor had left, he would be confined inside for a while.

Those three nights Leo slept badly. He was worried, but he also hoped very much that the operation would turn him into a real high wire artist like the other members of his family. Maybe even the best, the greatest acrobat of all. His father would be proud of him at last, and his mother wouldn't be so sad.

The great day arrived. Doctor Ermine turned up very early in the morning. Mr. Griffon had lit a fire in the workshop stove and he'd gone outside to remove the thin coating of snow that the wind had driven onto the glass roof. The lanterns were lit.

"There's no need to worry, child, we'll be right here with you as long as you need us."

As she did every morning, Ms. Melody had pinned the name of the day to her pocket. For this occasion, she also wore a nurse's bonnet which she had tied securely under her chin. Though it wasn't very large, embroidered on the top of the bonnet were a little spoon that held a mixture of something, and a green bottle. As for Mr. Griffon, he was the same as always. Nothing different, nothing changed. Leo was reassured.

As he prepared his instruments, Doctor Ermine talked softly to his patient. He explained that he would be shaving the hair from Leo's paw. Skilfully, he got down to work. Griffon and Melody were sitting beside Leo, close to the table. Leo lay on the workbench, resting on some big cushions. He was nervous. The doctor gave him an injection that took away all sensitivity in that part of his body. Ms. Melody had fixed him a hot drink to relax him. Leo sipped the mixture.

He could feel that the doctor was cutting into his skin, but he felt no pain. It was a strange experience. He tried to think about something else. Throughout the operation he didn't dare to look. What if he bled to death? He wouldn't admit it, but he felt quite uneasy.

Doctor Ermine used the lenses to help him see better. Now and then he asked Ms. Melody to sponge the wound or to bring some boiled water. Mr. Griffon stayed on his chair, not moving, next to Leo.

"Are you all right, youngster? It's nearly over now, right Doctor?"

"Yes. You're very brave, Leo Polatouche. Your toes aren't joined together anymore."

Leo clung to the thought of a new life. The operation lasted a little longer than an hourglass that marked the time for baking an acorn pie. When it was all over, Griffon picked Leo up in his arms and put him in his bed close to the fireplace. Melody helped the doctor clean up. They burned all the cloths that they'd used and washed the instruments. Leo sipped some more of the hot drink and drifted into a deep sleep. He didn't hear the doctor leave the moles' house.

CHAPTER 10

A Weight on the Heart

In the weeks that followed, Doctor Ermine visited several times. Leo was recovering quickly. He did exercises to stretch his tendon and to tone his muscles. Soon he was able to stand up and take a few steps around the table, supporting himself on the chairs.

He also had a wonderful experience. After the doctor had examined Leo, he joined the couple in the workshop. They were a team: Leo was able to help build and fine-tune a new sound for the forest harmonium.

Mr. Griffon had settled Leo on a big cushion on the workbench so that he could follow every stage in the work without getting tired. He had already brought up from the storeroom several reeds of different sizes. The team was working meticulously at producing the sound of crickets.

"The sounds of animals and insects are the hardest to make," said the doctor. "Here are the sound sensors, Griffon."

Over the weeks Ms. Melody had woven, braided, and embroidered the sound sensors. Doctor Ermine said again with great conviction: "You have to let nature inspire you."

Which was what they'd done. Ms. Melody had made some small woven objects that looked like spider webs, while others suggested the cells of a beehive, and others still resembled long water weeds.

With infinite patience, working under a lens, Mr. Griffon fastened together several layers of webs and cells. He combined a number of components at different heights inside the reed that he'd chosen.

The doctor was very helpful because of his good eyesight, and with his long surgical instruments, he could go very deep inside the pipes. At each stage the sound was tested and measured. Ms. Melody had a very good ear.

As they had done many times before, they now used the valves and keys to produce the desired length and variations of the sound. A few days later, when their "cricket song" had been perfected, Mr. Griffon closed the reed at one end and the bellows at the other. The new sound took its place in the forest harmonium. Ms. Melody could now work it into her compositions.

To pass the time, Leo drew and he talked a lot with Mr. Griffon, who brought him to the workshop every day. At first, he carried Leo in his arms, or pushed him on the wheeled chair. Sometimes he gave Leo a ride on his back.

Later on, Leo didn't need help. He supported himself on the furniture. But oddly enough, the stronger Leo became, the worse he felt. The moles had been so kind and gentle with him, and he was now very fond of them. The terrible secret and guilt he had carried through the winter weighed heavily on his mind. One morning he dared to ask:

"Mr. Griffon. If I told you I had lied to you, would you think I'm bad?"

"Not at all. I would try to understand why you hadn't told the whole truth — why you needed to hide some things from us. Would telling the truth be all that hard, Leo?"

Out it came in a rush. "I was very angry at my parents. I wanted to punish them so I left the houseboat. I really did fall asleep. When I woke up in the morning the house was gone. And the accident afterwards . . . I'm afraid that it was all my fault. They were coming back to find me, but now, because of me, they might be dead."

"Do you think that your anger could trigger something that terrible? No, child, there was more anger and misfortune inside of you than outside. Don't despair. Spring is coming. Maybe we'll hear something hopeful. Meanwhile, get better and keep drawing."

Tears poured down Leo's cheeks. He couldn't stop crying. Mr. Griffon's kind words made him sob twice as hard. Would they let him stay with them forever if his family didn't want him back? And if his family wasn't alive, what would they do with him? The future was full of uncertainty.

After hearing this outburst of sorrow, Mr. Griffon put down his plane and sat on a little bench a short distance away. Then he got up and laid his heavy paw on Leo's shoulder for a moment.

"Are you going to tell Ms. Melody?" Leo asked.

"Whatever you like, child."

"I don't want to tell her."

"All right, it will be our secret for as long as you say. Now blow your nose. If Melody sees you in this state, she'll think that you're sick or that I've upset you."

During the days that followed this conversation, Leo used the time he spent in the workshop with Mr. Griffon to talk freely and to enjoy his company. By doing things with Mr. Griffon, Leo was learning.

Three weeks after the surgery he was able to walk again, and to wash the lenses. He had resumed going outside, but he wasn't climbing trees yet. Everything was brand new for him: he balanced himself and walked differently now. His body seemed to be supported properly on his legs. In the evenings, at the end of each day, he massaged his paw and his toes with one of Ms. Melody's oils. The little incisions were healing well and his fur was growing back.

The exercises on the harmonium were

very good for Leo's paw because he had to press his feet on the bellows to drive air into the pipes. He had become quite good at pulling the keys that opened and closed the valves. However, fairly often he still cut off the sound too abruptly.

Ms. Melody was a real champion. When she played, the whole forest came into their underground home. She didn't just make sounds the way Leo did. Ms. Melody knew how to *play*. Every day while Leo had been convalescing, she gave him a little concert. In that way she made up for the fact that Leo couldn't go outside to hear the familiar sounds. He sat next to her or stretched out in his soft little bed to savour and name every one of the combinations.

CHAPTER 11

Big News!

Winter was nearly over. The days were getting longer. The sun was warmer. They no longer had to take the snow off the glass roof; little by little it melted by itself.

Mr. Griffon was looking forward to the return of the newspaper, which always came with the return of spring and the thaw. Spring would also bring news from the family of Leo Polatouche. There was a feeling of change and excitement in the air. Not much was said about the possibility that Leo might leave, but there were times when

Ms. Melody would impulsively put her paw on Leo's little shoulder. Just like that — but for no clear reason.

On days that were grey but warm, and the sun wasn't too hard on her eyes, Melody would go outside with Griffon and Leo for a brief time. The Magpie arrived on one of those grey days, proclaiming the news. All excited, she cried at the top of her lungs: "The Polatouche family is alive, the houseboat will go back in the water!"

The news was so sudden and so wonderful that Leo almost collapsed with relief. Ms. Melody, strangely quiet, held him close until he was steadier on his feet. Mr. Griffon winked a moist eye behind his thick spectacles. "There you go, child. You see? There was reason to hope after all."

It had been a break in the rudder that caused the accident. All winter the family had taken refuge with some distant cousins — a family of chipmunks. They would soon get back on the water road and resume the search for their son. The rudder had been repaired and the refitting had begun. Leo was very familiar with all the maintenance work that was needed so that come spring, their floating house would be shipshape.

Leo was going to see his family again: his grandfather, his mother, his brothers and sisters. But he would also have to face his father, explain to him, apologize. He passed from joy to anxiety in just a few minutes. It was something very hard to imagine.

Ms. Melody made a quick decision. She had to prepare their baggage for a day of travelling. They would dress properly for the trip, and they'd take food and Leo's things in a little cart. They would go to meet Leo's family. There. It was said.

They had to wait another two long weeks. The forest paths weren't suitable for vehicles. Moreover, they needed all that time to sort out Leo's things: his drawings

— he'd done a lot; his pencils, pens, colours; his clothes; an hourglass (a gift from Mr. Griffon); and some badges that named the days of the week and showed the weather conditions (a gift from Ms. Melody).

All three of them had trouble imagining their separation, although the time for it had come. Leo prepared a gift for the moles as well. He made a charcoal drawing of the three of them together. His best drawing. As well, on the family tree staircase he carved his name on a little branch, as if he were Mr. Griffon's and Ms. Melody's son. A little branch right next to the one for Scribble and Dawn.

On the last night he had a dream: he was a flying squirrel, but he had the wings of a bat. He flew freely, held up by the wind beneath his wings. The sensation was even more fantastic than walking on the wire or jumping. He was flying in a gentle mist. He had touched down in a nest at the top of a tree, a nest that was all round and cozy, and he fell into a peaceful sleep.

With their preparations finished, they left the next day at dawn. The couple walked slowly. Each of them had brought a hat with a visor and tinted magnifying lenses. The light was very bright. The wind was blowing. Grandfather, with his hands in his pockets, chest swollen, and muzzle to the wind, would have said that it was blowing away the winter. In the undergrowth there was still a lot of snow, but in other places it had disappeared. There was the smell of damp earth and the sound of water dripping. Along the way the moles picked up some small objects that might come in handy. Leo ran ahead of them, then retraced his steps, and climbed trees to see the stream. He was very excited.

They stopped once to rest and eat their

lunch. With the little cart, walking was difficult. At last they were on the path next to the stream.

"Mr. Griffon, are we going to go to the place where we performed the last show?"

"No, youngster, that's already behind us. We went past it in the forest."

The path bore the marks of winter and it had not yet been tamped down by the comings and goings of small forest animals. Then there was the baggage. Mr. Griffon and Ms. Melody were tired. They often leaned their backs against a tree to catch their breath.

By mid-afternoon they were finally at a spot where there was a clearing on the shoreline of the small river. There, before them, was the floating house moored in a cove. An adult Polatouche had his back to them as he busily scrubbed the hull of the boat. It was Leo's father. Mr. Griffon and Ms. Melody stopped as Leo rushed forward.

"Papa, Papa!"

Mr. Polatouche turned around and saw Leo.

"My little Leo! Marguerite, Marguerite! He's back!"

He embraced Leo.

"Papa, Papa, I'm sorry."

"So am I, dear child."

Mr. Polatouch held his son tight in his arms. Marguerite came running along with the rest of the family. They bombarded Leo with questions, they patted him, kissed him, shook him. It was a grand celebration.

"Grandpa — where's Grandpa?"

"Don't worry, Grandpa's fine. He went out to look for resin for caulking the boat."

The moles had stayed off to one side. Leo led them to his parents and formally introduced everyone.

"Mr. Griffon and Ms. Melody, I would like to introduce my father, Leonid Polatouche, and my mother, Marguerite Polatouche. These are my brothers, Farrago and Farrier, and my sisters, Jasmine, Violet, Rose, and Petunia."

They brought out a table and chairs from the floating house. Marguerite offered tea and cookies. They settled on the shore, as Ms. Melody and Mr. Griffon preferred solid ground. Leo left the adults together. They talked for a long time. They looked at his drawings, spoke about the operation, and told a little about their lives.

Leo watched his parents out of the corner of his eye: their reactions to the words, to the drawings that Griffon and Melody presented to them. Now and then their eyes met and Leo noticed a look of wonder on their faces that he'd never seen before.

The relief was tremendous. The moles said only what was necessary, essential. The rest was private: the secret time of Leo Polatouche the Acrobat, of Ms. Melody, and of Mr. Griffon.

Leo was reconnecting with his past life.

He went all over the houseboat, top to bottom and up and down, with his brothers and sisters. He rediscovered his bed and the familiar aromas: of his mother, of clothes, of their house. There were so many new things to talk about. His family, too, had spent a very unusual winter.

He was struck by the vast difference between the lives of the moles and those of the flying squirrels. For the moles, everything was muffled, slow, silent, while in his family, it was exuberance, running, and noise. That night, before they left, Leo hugged the moles. Ms. Melody gave him a farewell souvenir: seven little handkerchiefs with their initials in delicate embroidery. She had put them in a little box with some cedar chips.

"If you can," she said, "please keep in touch with us. We'll never forget you, Leo."

"That's right," Griffon agreed.

Leo's family had offered to put the moles up for the night, but Griffon and Melody preferred to leave, even if it meant looking for a shelter for the night. *Certainly not in a floating house*, they thought.

The Polatouche family went to bed very late that night. They had a lot of things to say and to explain. Leo had climbed onto his grandfather's back, holding on tight to his neck as he'd done so many times before, when Grandpa would sit in his big chair. He showed his toes and the barely visible scar on his paw. He described the moles' house and they told him about where the chipmunks lived. They all felt as if they had escaped a very great danger. They all had a greater understanding of the fragility of things. They were happy.

The next spring, Griffon and Melody received, via the Magpie, a poster advertising a show by the Polatouche family. At the

bottom of the poster, paintbrush in hand, was Leo, offering to paint the spectators' portraits.

Now and then, Leo liked to drop in on the moles when the houseboat was in their vicinity. At other times, when the Magpie dropped by, he would send them a message. The winter he'd spent underground with Griffon and Melody had transformed Leo.

He never became a greater acrobat than he had ever been. Still, he no longer fell from the high wire. He enjoyed climbing up there for his own pleasure, but he liked drawing better. His father understood. Leo had a full life. Sometimes he even dreamed that one day he would find a house on terra firma.